# Little Little Sister

*To Cassie*
J.L.C.

*To little little Kaye*
E.B.

*Jane Louise Curry*

# Little Little Sister

*Illustrated by*
*Erik Blegvad*

MARGARET K. McELDERRY BOOKS • NEW YORK

Margaret K. McElderry Books
Macmillan Publishing Company
866 Third Avenue
New York, NY 10022
Collier Macmillan Canada, Inc.

First Edition
Printed in Hong Kong by South China Printing Co.
10  9  8  7  6  5  4  3  2  1

Library of Congress Cataloging-in-Publication Data
Curry, Jane Louise.
Little little sister.
Summary: Little Sister, a tiny girl who grows from
an apple seed, helps her brother get home safely each
time he strays on an errand in the wide world.
[1. Fairy tales]  I. Blegvad, Erik, ill.
II. Title.
PZ8.C936Li  1989    [E]      88-13079
ISBN 0-689-50459-4

Once upon a while ago, not so very long ago—and far away, but not so far that you couldn't walk there in a week or so—there lived a farmer and his wife.

They lived in a house at the foot of the mountains, under a broad oak tree in the middle of a fine field beside a wide river. The house was small, but not too small, and they thought themselves rich, for they had a little barn and an apple tree,

and a horse for ploughing the field,

a brown cow for milking,

six sheep for shearing,

ten red hens for laying eggs,

a cock for crowing,

a cat for ratting,

and a brave dog for barking.

Best of all, they had a fine son to gather the eggs—unless he forgot; to carry the pail of milk from the cow to the kitchen—though sometimes he spilled it; and to feed the horse his hay—which he did very well when he remembered.

"What more could we wish for!" said the proud farmer each night after supper as he leaned back in his chair and lit his pipe.

"Not a thing, unless it be fair skies tomorrow," said his wife each night if the day had been cloudy. When the days were hot and dry she said instead, "Unless it be a good rain tomorrow."

And every evening when the wife made her answer, the son looked up from whittling a new flute or whistle and added, "Or a nice little sister."

Then the farmer would sigh.

And his wife sighed too.

For they were growing older, and had given up hope of another child to share their pride in the fine horse and cow and sheep and hens, and their pleasure in the house and dog and cat.

"Too late for that," said the farmer each night with a shake of his head.

"Too late," his wife agreed with a sigh.

And their son turned back to his whittling.

That winter was deep and hard. The river froze. Snow fell all day, every day. It fell and fell until it was heaped as high as the farmhouse eaves. And because the barn was too far for the farmer to go in the cold and snow to feed them, the horse and cow and sheep and chickens stayed snug indoors with the farmer and his wife and son and the dog and cat.

The animals dozed all day each day. The farmer sharpened his plough by the fire. Or cleaned his boots. His wife spun wool into yarn. Or knitted it into socks. Their son whittled a little wooden ball for the cat to play with. Or a spoon for stirring the soup.

On one such day the farmer set to mending the horse's harness. His wife sorted apples to slice into rings to hang from the rafters to dry, and their son whittled rods to hang them on.

After supper that evening the farmer leaned back in his chair and lit his pipe. "Come, now! What more could we wish for?" he said as before.

"Not a thing," his wife replied. "Unless it be bright skies tomorrow."

But just then, as their son was about to wish the wish for a little sister that he always wished, the horse neighed, the cat sat up and meowed, and the dog spoke, plain as plain.

"Put up your knife, good wife," said he. "That apple's not for slicing."

"Well," said she, "that's fine with me. I'll eat it myself."

And she did, and spat the seeds into a saucer and ate the core, and thought no more about it, but went to hang her apple rings to dry. The horse went back to sleep, the cat yawned, and the dog stretched out in front of the fire without another word.

The next morning, the son rose at cock-crow. When he climbed down from the loft, the horse and cow and sheep and cock and hens and cat and dog still were fast asleep. But the farmer and his wife stood peering down at the saucer that sat on the table.

"My, oh!" exclaimed the farmer. And he beckoned to his son. "Come see!"

"My, oh indeed!" said the farmer's wife. "Come see what has grown from the apple seed!"

The son's eyes grew round, and his mouth made an O of surprise. For there in the saucer, fast asleep, lay a baby no bigger than a newborn mouse. He bent close to touch one tiny foot with a careful finger.

"Little sister!" said he. "*Little* little sister."

And he clapped his hands for happiness. "What could we wish for now?" he cried. "Not a thing in this world. Not a single thing!"

He carved a fine cradle for Little Sister. And a box with a lid for the blankets his mother wove from the finest wool. And a handle for a tiny seed-pod rattle.

And year by year Little Sister grew—though not very much. Brother did not care about that. He thought there could be no one so pretty, no one so dainty, in all the wide world. He whittled her a birchwood bed, and a cherrywood chair. He whittled a little oaken table and carved applewood plates and a cherrystone cup, so that Little Sister could sit at her own place atop the big table when they all sat down to supper. Brother fetched this for her and made that for her, whatever might please her or keep her safe.

He saved nine silver pennies to buy her a tiny silver spoon. He made a box like a little room with a door and windows, so that if she were alone in the house she could shut herself safe away from the cat. Then he saved six silver pennies more, to buy a collar with a bell for the cat to wear.

But Little Sister liked the cat. She played ball with her. She rode on the dog's back. She was afraid of nothing and curious about everything, most of all about the river and field and all the wide world outside the cottage.

"No, no," said the farmer. "The wide world is a dangersome place, my dumpling."

"Indeed it is," agreed his wife.

"I'll carve you a boat to sail in the sink," said Brother, "and plant you a windowbox with moss for grass, and a wee little tree."

The wee little tree was very nice.

And every morning when Brother went out to do his chores, Little Sister sat under its branches to watch out the window and wonder about the wide, wide world.

One morning each week the farmer and his wife walked to the village to sell their eggs and milk and cheeses. Brother stayed home to plough and harrow and sow and weed the field beside the river. On one such morning the horse fell lame, and Brother went off and away to the crossroads atop the hill beyond the wood behind the field, to buy a pot of liniment from the little old woman who lived there. "I'll be back in no time at all," said he.

But the morning passed. Brother did not come back, and did not come back. At last Little Sister put on her cloak and her wooden clogs, and slipped out through a hole only she and the cat knew of. The cat went along to show her the way. Some of the time Little Sister rode on the cat's back. Some of the time she walked.

The shadows grew long and the sun slipped down behind the tall trees. Still Little Sister saw no sign of Brother, but she was not really sorry, for though the road was rough and the way long, the breeze was fresh and the wide world very beautiful.

"Have you seen my brother pass by?" she asked of all she met on the road. "He is tall as tall and good as gold."

"Not I," buzzed the beetle and the bumblebee.

"Not we," piped the puddleful of tadpoles.

"Perhaps," said the little red squirrel. "If it is he who sits under the crossroads tree eating the poppyseed cakes."

And it was. For the old woman's cakes were warm from the oven and light as air, so that Brother had forgotten his errand and stayed and played on his flute all the afternoon to earn another taste, and still another. Only when he spied Little Sister and the cat stepping up the road did he see how long the shadows were. He thrust his flute in one pocket, the pot of liniment in another, and Little Sister in a third, and ran all the way home.

"Never again!" said the farmer when he heard what Little Sister had done. "The wide world is no place for you, my cabbage."

"No indeed," agreed his wife. "And the cat should have warned you so," said she.

"I'll board up the cat's hole," promised Brother. "And I'll not forget to come home again. Not ever."

But he did.

On the very next market day, no sooner were the farmer and his wife off and away to town than the horse cast a shoe while ploughing. So what could Brother do but unharness him and lead him up and away to the blacksmith for a new one?

The clouds blew away and the day grew warm, and by noonday Brother still had not returned. At last Little Sister tied on her bonnet and drew on her clogs, and slipped out under the door. The dog barked a warning, but when Little Sister said, "Come," he fell into step beside her. They walked and they walked. They passed the crossroads and the old woman's house, and as they went, the sun grew so hot that the still air shimmered and Little Sister began to wilt. But still she would not turn back, so the dog walked above her like a four-legged parasol and she was cool in his shadow.

"Have you seen my brother?" Little Sister asked everyone they passed. "He is tall as tall, and as true as steel."

"No," said the snail and the earthworm.

"Not today," said the tortoise.

"Perhaps," said the toad, "if he's sitting by the blacksmith's shed down the road, drinking cider."

And he was. For the blacksmith's yard was shady, his cider sweet and cool. And his anvil made such a merry *cling-clang!* that Brother had stayed and played his flute to it all the afternoon. Only when he spied Little Sister trudging up the road in the little dog's shadow did Brother think of the lateness of the hour. He put Little Sister in his shirt pocket, broke off a leafy branch to shade them from the sun, leaped up onto the new-shod horse, and trotted briskly home.

"Bless me," said the farmer when he heard of it. "It seems the wide world is no place for either of you."

"Indeed it's not," agreed his wife, "and the dog should have told you so."

Poor Brother was as sorry as he was warm and sweaty. "On my conscience, I'll never, *never* forget to come home again," said he.

"You will," said Little Sister.

"Won't," said Brother.

But he did.

One market day not long afterward, the farmer fell ill. So he sent Brother to market in his place, to sell the brown cow's daughter. Brother clapped on his hat and set off proudly. The sun shone, the heifer trotted as obediently at Brother's side as if he were the farmer himself, and Little Sister was safe and snug at home.

Or so Brother thought.

At the crossroads atop the hill he slowed, remembering the taste of the old woman's poppyseed cakes.

"To market, to market!" called a small, gruff voice. It sounded a very little bit like Little Sister, but she of course was snug at home and her voice was not at all gruff. Brother decided it was his conscience telling him not to dawdle. So on he strode with the heifer at his heels until he came to the blacksmith's, and heard the merry *cling-clang!* of the anvil. Remembering the taste of the blacksmith's cider, he slowed.

"To market, to market," cried the small, gruff voice. So Brother, feeling quite proud of his conscience, marched briskly past the blacksmith's shed, the heifer trotting behind.

At the market square in the town, many farmers admired the heifer. "I'll give three crowns," said one. Brother grinned and would have agreed, for three crowns were three gold coins more than his pocket had ever seen.

"Too little," said the small, gruff voice.

"Too little," echoed Brother, changing his smile to a frown.

"Five crowns," offered another.

"Too little," warned the voice.

"Aye, too little," said Brother.

The heifer was sold at last for nine gold pieces, and Brother was mightily pleased with himself and his conscience. So pleased was he that he bought a beef pie and a bowl of milk, and sat himself down at the roadside, never spying how dark with clouds the sky had grown.

"There!" said the small voice before he could eat a bite. "I knew it. You'll be late home again. And I smell rain!"

"What a fine conscience I have!" cried Brother, jumping up. "I knew it would not let me forget to go home again."

He drank up his milk, wrapped the pie in his handkerchief, popped it into his pocket, and set off for home as fast as his feet knew how. Little Sister—for the small voice was indeed her—Little Sister and the pie bounced and jounced along together. She began to wish she had chosen another pocket to ride to market in.

The lightning flickered and the thunder rolled.

The wind snatched off Brother's hat and sent it on before him. The rain clouds raced after him as he ran.

Soon fat drops plopped on Brother's head. They dropped one by one at first, and then by dozens and hundreds. *Split-splat-split-splat!* And then they poured down like a waterfall. *SHROO-OO-OOMSH!*

Rainwater rushed over the ground, and down the road in a river. It filled Brother's boots, and went *swulsh-slosh, swulsh-slosh* as he ran.

"Hurry! Hurry!" cried a small, gruff voice as Brother passed the blacksmith's shed.

"I am, I am!" panted Brother to himself. But just then a long, dark shape came bobbing along the rushing, rivery road and knocked him heels over head.

"Catch it! Catch it!" Little Sister called as Brother picked himself up, for the long dark shape was the drinking trough for the horses the blacksmith shod.

"I will, I will!" cried Brother as he ran after the trough.

When he caught it, Brother lifted it and poured out the water, for he was very strong.

"What a good idea I have!" said he to himself. "And I'll take the trough back to the blacksmith tomorrow." Whereupon he climbed in and skimmed away down the road in the drinking trough.

Little Sister stood on the meat pie, the better to see out from Brother's pocket as they sailed downhill on the rivery road. All there was to see of the valley below were raindrops, treetops, and water, for the rain had filled the wide river and spilled over its banks. It slid across the meadows and swallowed up the old farmer's field. Only the hedgetops showed where the field began.

At the bottom of the hill, as the horse trough sailed along beside the hedge, Brother stood up, the better to see.

The farmhouse sat safe atop its hummock. But alas! The barn stood window-deep in water. Little Sister heard the old horse neigh and the brown cow moo. The cock and the ten red hens huddled on the henhouse roof.

"The sheep! The sheep!" shouted Little Sister, spying six twitching noses and six pairs of wild black eyes crowded together against the hedge.

*Beh-eh-eh! Beh-eh-eh!* the silly sheep bleated.

"Hold fast! Hold fast!" bellowed Brother as the trough sailed on toward the gate. In no time at all he was hip-deep in the water, and soon had the six sopping sheep stowed safely in the horse trough.

"The roof! The roof!" cried the little little voice.

"What a fine idea, my good conscience!" said Brother. "The rain is still raining and the river still rising, so I will put the sheep on the roof. They are sure to be safe up there."

And once the sheep were safe on the farmhouse roof, Brother went to the barn to bring the horse and cow, and then to the henhouse for the cock and the hens. After he had put them all up to roost beside the sheep, he opened the farmhouse door and strode in proudly.

"Do you see, dear Father?" said he. "I came straight home as my conscience told me, and I have saved our six silly sheep from drowning, and put all of the animals safe on the roof."

But the farmer only groaned and turned his face to the wall. His wife wept behind her apron.

"What is all that to us," sobbed she, "when Little Sister is lost in the storm, drowned and swept down to the sea?"

"But I'm not! I'm not!" cried Little Sister from atop the pie in Brother's deep shirt pocket.

At that, the farmer leaped from his sickbed to dance a jig for joy with his wife. Brother was so pleased that Little Sister had not been drowned and swept down to the sea that he did not care in the least that it was she who had brought him safely home and not his fine conscience at all.

The farmer marveled at the nine gold coins Brother gave him. And when he had heard the whole of it, he shook his head. "The wide world may be no place for either of you alone," he said, "but together you do very well."

"And so they do," his wife agreed.

So from that day on, every week on market day, Brother carried the eggs and milk and cheeses to market, Little Sister sold them for the very best price, and the farmer and his wife stayed at home and blessed the day the clever dog said, "That apple's not for slicing."